Banding Together

Story by Janeen Brian
Illustrations by Christine Luiten

NELSON
A Cengage Company

Banding Together

Text: Janeen Brian
Series consultant: Annette Smith
Publishing editor: Simone Calderwood
Editor: Annabel Smith
Designer: Kerri Wilson
Series designers: James Lowe and
    Karen Mayo
Illustrations: Christine Luiten
Production controller: Erin Dowling
Reprint: Siew Han Ong

PM Guided Reading
Ruby Level 28

Gadget Girl
Special Effects: Bringing Movies to Life
Banding Together
Play On!
The Power of Wind
Time and Clocks
Amazing Stories of Survival
Wildfire
Southern Skies
Shipwrecked!

Text © 2016 Cengage Learning Australia Pty Limited
Illustrations © 2016 Cengage Learning Australia Pty Limited

ISBN 978 0 17 037307 4

Cengage Learning Australia
Level 7, 80 Dorcas Street
South Melbourne, Victoria Australia 3205
Phone: 1300 790 853

Cengage Learning New Zealand
Unit 4B Rosedale Office Park
331 Rosedale Road, Albany, North Shore NZ 0632
Phone: 0800 449 725

For learning solutions, visit **cengage.com.au**

Printed in Singapore by 1010 Printing Group Limited
4 5 6 7 20 19 18

Contents

Chapter 1   Leaving Home   5

Chapter 2   A New Start   14

Chapter 3   A Cruel Prank   22

Chapter 4   Homesickness   27

Chapter 5   A Glimmer of Hope   32

Chapter 6   Banding Together   37

Chapter 7   Talent Triumph   44

Chapter 1

Leaving Home

Joel stared down at the dusty roofs and houses from his window seat in the plane. It looked like a toy town. Surrounding the town was dry, desert land with a few short trees and winding roads like snakes.

"I hate it already," he murmured.

Toby, his seven-year-old brother, elbowed Joel out of the way for a closer look.

"Wow!" he said. "This is going to be great."

Joel slumped down in his seat. He wouldn't, couldn't share Toby's enthusiasm for their new home in the country.

When the plane finally landed, a chatty lady called Mary met Joel, Toby and their mum and dad at the airport and drove them to their furnished, rented house. Mary was from the local real-estate agency.

"All the belongings you sent have been stacked around the back. So I'll make you a nice cup of tea while you have a look around the house," said Mary.

It was the last thing Joel wanted to do. He scuffed down the narrow hall, barely casting a glance either side. At least he had a bedroom to himself. Nothing would be worse than sharing with Toby, who'd just learned to whistle and spoke to an imaginary friend.

Mum gave a polite smile as she walked from one small room to another. "It's lovely!" she proclaimed, accepting a cup of tea from Mary. "I'm sure we'll be happy here."

"It'll be good to have a local vet again," Mary said to Dad, with a welcoming smile. "It's been difficult for the farmers since the last one left. Anyway, I'll let you settle in. Anything you want, there's my number." She pointed to a piece of paper on the kitchen table.

Before heading out the back door, Mary turned to Joel. "So you'll be starting school on Monday, eh? Looking forward to it?" Before he could answer, Mary continued, "It'll be a bit different from your other school in the city, I suppose. Being a country school, we've got all ages, from prep to high school. And lots of kids come in on the school bus. They live out on sheep and cattle properties, so they're not all from the town. And my Chelsea's in your class." She smiled.

"I'm sure Joel will get used to it," said Joel's mum. "As will Toby. We'll be here for at least two years. Plenty of time."

Inside, Joel was seething. How did his mum know that he'd get used to it? It was just like an adult to say that. He'd been with the same schoolmates at St Benedict's since he first started school. Then, at the start of year 5, his dad had accepted a new job at a veterinary clinic at Wilchna, way out in the country, at least 20 kilometres from the next town.

For weeks, there'd been arguments about the departure. Joel had never felt so angry. Why did they have to move?

"You're being mean," Toby had said one day, after Joel had stormed out of the kitchen at their old home, slamming the door as he left. "It'll be good fun in the country!"

"Little kids like you don't understand," Joel muttered.

"I'm not that little," Toby answered, puffing out his chest. "Anyway, we might get a horse to ride."

As if that meant anything.

"You boys will be able to walk to school,"
said Dad that night, as he finished off some pie
that Mary had baked and left for them to heat up.
"That'll make a nice change from having to be
driven, eh?"

"I suppose so," said Joel. His mum had always
dropped him and Toby off and picked them up
again after school, and in between times, she worked
at home as a graphic artist.

"All that fresh air and exercise," added his mum.

Why didn't they just stop? Joel was sick of hearing about all the supposedly good things that were going to happen at the new place. What about all the good things that he was going to miss out on back at his old school? Football competitions, chess club, swimming carnivals and guitar lessons. Not to mention hanging out with his best mates, Harry, Sam, Jordan and Emil. Or his teacher, Mr Adams, who was funny and made schoolwork interesting.

"You can talk to your friends online, Joel," said Mum, as if she'd read his mind. "More pie?"

"No, thanks. Can I go now?" grumbled Joel.

"Clear your dishes," said Dad.

"Can I go, too?" said Toby.

"You're not coming with me," said Joel.

"Why, where are you going?" said Toby.

"My bedroom, and you're not invited."

"Shall I show you my horse drawing?"

"No."

Joel strode down the hall. He felt rotten. Toby wasn't such a bad brother, as far as little brothers went, but right now he wanted to be alone. He shut himself in his room and stood, arms hanging by his sides. All the smells were wrong. The curtains were flowery and dull. And they let in too much light.

Joel had brought some of his favourite books from home, but there was no proper shelf to put them on, just an old bedside table. As he was setting them up, his foot accidentally knocked his school backpack.

His mum had insisted he bring all his textbooks and exercise books. As well as his tablet, of course. They were using them a lot more now at St Benedict's. When Joel thought of not being there on Monday morning, a sick, hollow feeling filled his stomach. What would it be like walking into a new school, into an unfamiliar classroom filled with kids he didn't know? What would the teacher be like? Would he know the work?

A feeling of cold dread crept up his spine.

He undressed and got ready for bed. Night had come on quickly and soon there were so many stars shining through the gap in the middle of the curtains, he wondered if he'd ever sleep at all. He gave the curtains another yank, but they wouldn't budge. With a disgruntled sigh, he turned off the bedside light and climbed into bed.

A minute later, there was a faint knock at his door and a small voice called out "Postie!"

Toby!

"What do you want?" Joel demanded.

"Postie!" came the voice again, and then nothing.

Irritated, Joel flicked on the light and discovered a piece of paper that had been slipped under the door.

It was a drawing of a horse, and on its saddle, Toby had written "Silver Star".

Joel gave a wry smile and shook his head. He hesitated, wondering what to do with the drawing. There was no wastepaper basket in the room, so he shoved it between the pages of one of his books, to use as a bookmark.

Again, he tried to sleep.

Chapter 2

A New Start

Sunday disappeared in a whirl of unpacking and setting out a few things that made the new house feel more homely, as Mum said. But you can't just dump some cushions on a couch and say it feels like home, because it doesn't.

"Come outside and see the chickens," Toby called to Joel. "They're in a big wire pen and they're scratching in the dirt. I didn't know we'd have chickens, Dad!"

"We'll have fresh eggs, too," Mum called, in a cheery voice.

How come everyone else in the family felt as if this was one big, exciting adventure?

"See, Joel," Toby pointed out, "that chicken's got a long beak and that one's got a small beak. Which one do you want?"

"You can have them both."

"Wow! Thanks, Joel," cried Toby.

Joel knew he wasn't being generous. He simply couldn't care. Kicking at the dirt, he stared glumly around the backyard. It was edged in a plain iron fence, rusted in parts, with a scrap of yellowed lawn and a few dry-looking trees and bushes.

A thought leapt into Joel's mind. Did he have enough money saved to catch the next plane home?

Joel couldn't get out of it. The next day he was at the new school. His heart thumped as the teacher, Mrs Palomo, introduced him to the class of about fifteen kids, girls as well as boys. He stared at his feet, knowing his face was red. Why did he have to wear his old school shirt and long pants? Everyone else was in casual clothes.

"So, tell us about your hobbies, Joel," the teacher went on. "What do you like doing?"

Reluctantly, Joel raised his head.

A loud burp echoed through the classroom.

"Pardon!" said an equally loud voice. The class tittered. Joel's heart beat faster.

"Nathan!" snapped Mrs Palomo, glaring at a boy in the second row.

"I excused myself," the boy simpered. "I couldn't help it." A chuckle or two still rippled around the room.

"Quiet! What will Joel think of you all?"

Joel knew the answer to that question. *That you're a lot of country loudmouths and I don't even want to be here.*

"Your hobbies, Joel?" Mrs Palomo prompted, keeping a steely eye on Nathan. The boy was tapping his ruler against the edge of his desk, all the while grinning at Joel.

"I …" Joel began. But he paused. Why should he tell them what he liked doing? They weren't friends or mates. And that creep of a kid staring at him was like a lump of dough with a big mouth.

An uncomfortable silence filled the room. A couple of kids at the back nudged each other. A few began to whisper behind their hands. However, a girl down the front looked up at him. Her brows were furrowed, but she nodded with a small smile.

Joel took a breath.

"I like football, chess, swimming … and … a few other things," he ended lamely. He wasn't going to tell them about his guitar or his love of music. That was special to him, and he wasn't going to blurt it out like a kid in kindergarten.

Joel could tell that Mrs Palomo had been
expecting more, but when he stopped, she gave
a small murmur of interest and turned to face
the class.

Straightaway, the boy, Nathan, put down his ruler
and began to clap. Turning in his seat, he cheered
everyone on to join in. The clapping grew too loud
and went on for too long.

"Nathan!" The teacher strode up to the boy, who
upended his palms.

"I'm only saying welcome, Mrs Palomo."
His voice rose at the end and he blinked innocently,
as if puzzled by the teacher's reprimand.

Mrs Palomo paused and clasped her hands in front of her. "All right then," she said slowly, taking on a more polite, controlled tone. "Joel, you may sit here. This is Chelsea and Michaela and Dylan. They'll be very happy to help you find your way around the school."

The three kids turned to Joel as he made his way towards the empty seat at their desk. He dumped his St Benedict's monogrammed backpack on the floor.

"I'm Chelsea," said the girl who'd smiled before.

"Hi," he murmured. He set up an exercise book, a few pens and pencils, and his tablet on the desk.

"Lucky," said Chelsea, nodding towards the tablet.

Joel's eyes darted from side to side. Not another tablet in sight. He ground his teeth. Back to the dark ages!

The morning dragged on. Nathan constantly tapped the desk with either a pencil or a ruler, or thumped it with his palm. At the same time, he muttered punch-like sounds under his breath. Joel hunched forward in his seat, his skin prickling with irritation.

"Don't mind him," Chelsea whispered.

Easier said than done.

Chapter 3

A Cruel Prank

During recess and at the start of lunch, Chelsea, Michaela and Dylan strolled around the yard with Joel, occasionally pointing out particular school buildings or explaining what happened on certain days, such as Sports Day or Pets Day.

Joel nodded grudgingly, dismayed by the weathered classrooms, patchy football oval and the lack of a swimming pool.

A short time later, Chelsea checked her watch. "I'm on Buddy Alert," she said to Joel. "We each look after a little kid. When it's our turn, we play games with them or just check they're okay. See you." She turned and ran towards the playground.

"I'll be fine," Joel said hurriedly to the other two. "Don't worry about me."

"You sure?" asked Michaela.

"Yeah." Joel nodded, and Michaela and Dylan ran off as well.

Joel began to amble back towards the classroom, hoping to make himself as invisible as he could for as long as possible. As he mooched past a small room with a dusty window, a jumble of instruments caught his eye. What a mess. Drums, cymbals, trumpets and flutes lay discarded on shelves and benches. Music stands were pushed together in untidy heaps, and boxes with faded writing on them lay stacked about on the floor. It looked like no one had touched those instruments for months, maybe years. It wouldn't have surprised Joel if the door didn't even open.

So that was the school's music room. Remembering the music room back at St Benedict's made his heart sink. There, everything was shiny, tidy and well used. Miss Kemp, the music teacher, saw to that.

At that moment, when Joel thought things couldn't get any worse, a strong gust of wind swirled about the yard, blowing dust in his eyes and mouth. He wanted to spit. He wanted to cry out. He wanted to run away.

"Hi!" Nathan approached him like a loping bear. A grinning mate trudged alongside him. "How's it going, city-boy?" Nathan put one arm around Joel's shoulders and patted him heartily on the back. "Take care, won't you?" Then he and the other boy strode off. Joel blinked in shock.

As the bell sounded for the end of lunchtime, Joel had glimpsed a couple of kids pointing and whispering in his direction, but he'd slid his hands into his pockets and kept his head down, hating that he was the new boy.

Joel walked into the classroom, not looking at anybody. Just then, Chelsea rushed over and quickly pulled off a piece of paper stuck to his back. Joel looked at it and felt the blood rushing to his face.

"That was a rotten thing to do, Nathan Wilmot," Chelsea said, storming up to the boy.

Joel slid into his seat, mortified that a girl was standing up for him.

"Just a joke!" Nathan said. "Can't you take a joke?" The question was aimed bullseye at Joel.

The words bounced off his back but they still met their mark. His stomach churned. He hadn't laughed once since he'd arrived in Wilchna. And he couldn't see that he ever would.

Chapter 4

Homesickness

"Joel's always making me late for school," Toby groaned one night, a few weeks later, during dinner.

Joel shot him a glare.

"I am not."

"You are." Toby's voice rose. "You're always walking slowly. Like a zombie. And one day, you didn't even come into school with me."

"Be quiet!" Joel muttered under his breath, as he delivered a swift kick to Toby underneath the table.

"See, Mum! He's being mean again." Toby glared at Joel.

Joel pulled a face and moaned, mimicking his brother.

"That's enough, Joel," said Mum, glancing at Dad. Joel caught the exchange between his parents.

"Is that true, Joel? Were you late into school?" asked his mum.

Joel said nothing, remembering last Thursday morning. He and Toby had reached the school gate, but when Toby had run off with his friend, Joel quickly headed in the opposite direction. In a small park, he'd sat, knees hunched, until he'd picked a fingernail down clean to its edge. Then he'd dragged himself back towards the school gate. Once in the classroom, he'd made a feeble excuse to Mrs Palomo about returning home for a book. Then, eyes lowered, he'd slid into his seat.

"Joel," his mum went on, "we've been hearing worrying things about you from your teacher. Mrs Palomo is concerned that you're having trouble settling in."

"And," added his dad, "you're not finishing your work. And sometimes, you're not even handing it in."

Joel prodded a bit of broccoli with his fork.

"And I saw him push a big boy the other day," Toby added, wide-eyed, his voice a mixture of pride and alarm.

"All right, Toby," said Mum. "You go and find something to do."

"Does that mean I don't have to do the dishes?"

"Yes. Off you go," said Dad.

Joel raised his eyes as his brother sauntered past.

"So, Joel," said his mum, her voice softening. "Is there anything you'd like to talk about?"

Joel didn't know what to say. He hated being at the school. And Nathan made it worse. It was as if the boy spent hours thinking up new ways to disrupt the class. He had pretend coughing fits where he grasped his throat and rolled about wildly in his seat. He faked enormous sneezes and gave ridiculous answers to questions. Once, he made a loud bird noise, and then shouted, "Duck, everyone!" It took Mrs Palomo ages to control the laughter and settle the class back to their work.

No wonder Joel's schoolwork was hopeless. The classroom was like a circus at times. Plus, the work was different. His tablet with all his projects about the environment, famous musicians or inventions lay gathering digital dust in his backpack.

"Joel," said his dad, "tell us what's going on."

"Nothing, Dad," he replied, uneasily. "It's nothing." He was about to say how much he loathed being here, but he knew he'd get a sky-high lecture, so he shrugged again and stared at the mush he'd made of the broccoli.

"Give it time," said his mum, gently.

"You'll make friends," added his dad. "Why don't you invite some kids around here after school?"

"Maybe," said Joel, tasting the lie in his mouth.

His mum put her arms around him. "You're a good kid, Joel. Remember that."

Joel remained silent, but his palms were sweaty. Was that the end of it?

That night, Joel sat on his bed for a minute or two. Slowly, he reached beneath the bed and pulled out his guitar. Opening the case, he took the instrument in his hands and strummed a few chords.

It was the first time he'd played in a month. The notes went straight to his heart. He began to play some of the tunes he'd learned at St Benedict's, but then he added others, too, ones he'd taught himself.

He closed his eyes. Wilchna felt a world away.

Suddenly, there was a knock on the door.

"Go away, Toby!"

"Postie!" called the voice. A piece of paper slid under the door. Joel stretched his foot, dragged it back and read the note.

That big boy said you kissed a girl called Chelsea, but I don't believe him. Was it yucky?

Joel gave a cry of fury. He thrust the guitar back into its case and turned off his light.

Chapter 5

A Glimmer of Hope

Next morning, Joel set off for school, feeling as if his backpack was full of rocks. Toby prattled on annoyingly about his chickens and how he had two hardboiled eggs for lunch and was giving one to his friend, Niko.

Joel had other things on his mind. Toby's note burned in his brain. What if Nathan had already started a rumour that he'd kissed Chelsea?

He'd never be able to face going to school again.

Feeling sick to his stomach, Joel edged past the dusty music room and sat down at his desk. He drew his shoulders in tightly, longing to be invisible.

"Hi, Joel," said Chelsea, as she took her seat. She flicked her dark hair off her shoulders as usual, and then bustled about with her bag and books.

"Hi," he said tentatively.

"What have you been up to?" Chelsea asked.

Joel gulped. Was she trying to find out something?

"Nothing much," he said. And then, without meaning to, the words slipped out. "I played my guitar a bit last night."

Chelsea spun around to face him. Her eyes widened and she opened her mouth to say something, when Mrs Palomo clapped her hands for silence.

The hours crawled by. Joel buried his head to shut out Nathan's continual mutterings and comments. He gritted his teeth to finish work that he'd already done at St Benedict's, and his head spun. Should he say something to Nathan about Toby's note or not?

What if Toby had made it up? Somehow, as much as his brother liked to pretend with his imaginary friend, he didn't think Toby would've come up with a message like that on his own.

But … it was possible. What should he do?

Was Nathan laughing at him behind his back right now?

Joel couldn't wait for recess. He just wanted to get outside and clear his head. Part of him wondered, too, what Chelsea had been going to say to him earlier. As he tossed a banana skin into the bin, someone suddenly pushed the lid down and pinned his hand to the rim.

"Hey!" he cried, and turned to see the grinning face of Nathan.

"What?" Nathan kept his hand on the lid. "What's the matter?"

Joel tried to drag his hand free, scraping his skin along the edge of the bin. "You!" he said, jutting his jaw. "You're the matter!"

Joel was about to push Nathan with his free arm, when Chelsea appeared alongside.

"Come on, Joel," she said, grabbing his arm. "I've got something to show you."

Nathan let go and Joel allowed himself to be dragged away, flinching at the sound of the wolf whistles that rang out behind him.

Chelsea barged on, pulling Joel towards the school noticeboard. "Forget Nathan," she said. "It's better if you do."

"Why is it better?" he demanded. "Why is he like this? I've done nothing to him!"

Ignoring Joel's outbursts, Chelsea pointed to a big poster, recently pinned on the board. "Read that," she said. Her voice bubbled with excitement.

> ## WILCHNA COMMUNITY TALENT COMPETITION.
> ## PRIZES TO BE WON!
> ### ENTER NOW!

Joel stared at it blankly. "What about it?" he said.

"I sing. You play the guitar." She continued to stare at him, her eyes flickering with anticipation.

"No!" Joel cried, shaking his head. "No way. Not me!"

He turned to walk away.

"Okay, okay," Chelsea said. "We'll get someone else as well. Someone who's a good drummer."

"Who?"

"Nathan," she said.

Joel's mouth dropped open. "What?"

Chapter 6

Banding Together

"Your mum and I have come up with an idea, Joel," said his dad that night after dinner.

Joel flopped into an armchair, dreading what it might be.

"We thought you could have a sleepover here, next Friday night. You and all your friends could pitch tents out the back."

"And," added his mum, "we could have a barbecue and –"

"What?" Joel sat bolt upright. "Who?"

"We thought you could invite your whole class, and we'd have a campfire and –"

"Can we toast marshmallows, Mum?" cried Toby, leaping up from the floor, where he'd been drawing.

Joel's voice cracked. His eyes stung. "NO!" he cried at his parents. "NO!"

"Why not, Joel?" said his dad. "Wouldn't it be fun?"

"No, it wouldn't!" Joel jumped up and began to pace the room. "It's the last thing I'd want. We wouldn't do it for a whole class at St Benedict's. So why do it here?" He almost spat the last word.

"Can we still have marshmallows?" said Toby, looking eagerly first at his mum and then at his dad.

Joel strode into his bedroom, locked the door and stuffed the sleeve of his jacket into the gap between the door and the floor, so that no paper could slide through. Picking up his guitar, he began to strum hard on the strings. Slowly, his heart stopped pounding. He played until his eyes drooped.

Chelsea was waiting for him at the school gate the next morning. He couldn't dodge her.

"Joel?" Her face was set.

"What?" he muttered, trying to walk ahead.

"You have to know a few things about Nathan."

"No, I don't."

Chelsea quickened her pace.

"Nathan's mum died last year in a shop fire."

The words punched him in the chest, but he kept walking.

"Not only that, our music teacher left about the same time, because the school didn't get enough funding. And Nathan's dad hasn't got any money for drum lessons."

Joel slowed down.

"Okay," he said. "But he's still a pain."

Chelsea looked at him. "He wasn't always," she said.

Joel didn't know what to say.

"We could do it!" Chelsea went on. "The competition isn't until next week. It'd be fun! Nathan's different when he's drumming. We could come over to your place this afternoon to practise."

"What?"

"Why not?" She grinned.

The bell sounded and they headed off to class.

After school that day, Nathan and Chelsea arrived at Joel's front door. Chelsea was carrying a big folder, and Nathan was loaded down with drumming equipment.

"Hi," said Joel, stepping aside to let them in.

"Hi to you too." Chelsea breezed through.

"Hi," grunted Nathan.

Joel showed them into the lounge room, but kept his eye on Nathan. The scrape on the back of his hand was still sore. Once he'd introduced Chelsea and Nathan to his mum, they set up their equipment. Toby sat on a stool, looking on and clutching a chicken.

Chelsea gave a dramatic cough.

"Okay," she said, grinning. "Let's start. What songs do you know, Joel?"

"What songs do you know?" he replied.

Chelsea laughed and Joel surprised himself by giving a chuckle.

In the end, they settled on four songs they thought could work. "Let's get going, then," said Nathan. He picked up his drumsticks while Joel gave his guitar a final tune.

Inside, Joel was still dumbfounded. Was this kid, Nathan, the same pain that sat behind him at school? It was as if someone had done an unbelievable swap.

"One, two, three, four!" Nathan tapped them in and they began the first song. It didn't take long before Joel realised Chelsea was right. Nathan's hands were magic. He was a good drummer.

At the end of an hour, they sat down and talked about what they'd done, over a snack and a drink that Joel's mum had prepared.

"I think the first two songs are sounding good already," said Chelsea.

"But will we be good enough to win a competition?" said Joel.

"I could join in!" cried Toby.

Joel laughed, but Nathan said, "Hey, that's a New Hampshire chicken you've got there. Does she lay?"

Toby's head wobbled back and forth as if it was on a spring. "Every day!" he said. And then he beamed at Nathan as if the boy was suddenly a super-chicken-hero.

Chelsea counted off the days. "Six more days of practice. Is it all right if we come here each time, Joel?"

"Yeah," Joel said.

"Of course," agreed his mum.

"Okay?" said Chelsea again.

"Okay," Joel and Nathan chorused together and then gave an embarrassed grin.

For Joel, the following six days rushed by. He couldn't wait for the afternoons so they could practise their music.

The walk to school was getting easier. He was starting to know a few more of his classmates, the oval no longer seemed an unfriendly space full of strange faces, and even Nathan appeared to have other things on his mind apart from always being the class clown.

Chapter 7

Talent Triumph

At their final practice, they faced one last problem. What to call themselves?

Chelsea gave the first suggestion, which was "The Wilchna Trio".

Joel twisted his mouth. Wasn't it a bit boring?

"It says where we come from," said Chelsea.

"And," added Nathan, "it says that there are three of us."

After that, for some reason, Joel liked it.

The following afternoon, the Wilchna Trio was on stage at the Wilchna Community Hall in front of a hundred people, including Joel's mum and dad and Toby, Chelsea's mum, Mrs Palomo and many kids from school.

Joel stared out at the sea of smiling faces, at the hall decorated with streamers and balloons, at the rays of sun glinting through the tall windows, and his heart beat with a strange new feeling.

"Take it away, The Wilchna Trio!" enthused the announcer, walking off stage.

There was a round of applause, and Joel grinned at his parents and Toby, who were seated right up the front.

Nathan tapped them in with his drumsticks, and soon the music swept through the hall. Chelsea's clear, warm voice rang out, and Joel couldn't remember when he'd ever played his guitar better. After their four songs, they took a bow and walked off.

In the wings, they punched their fists in the air, grins stretching from ear to ear.

Finally, all the acts were over and the announcer stood in the middle of the stage with an envelope in his hand.

"The winner of the Wilchna Community Talent Competition is … Amelia Tan on piano!"

Joel felt a sick thud in his stomach. He raised his eyebrows at the other two.

"Oh, well," he began.

"Along with joint winners," continued the announcer, "The Wilchna Trio!"

"What?" cried Joel, as a swell of applause reached his ears.

Chelsea hugged both him and Nathan.

"We did it! We did it!" she cried.

"Now, let's eat!" said Nathan, eyeing the tables at the back of the hall. They groaned with pizzas, sandwiches, salads, cakes and fruit.

That night, Joel sat with his fifty-dollar share of the prize money. It had been one of the best days of his life.

His dad sat down alongside him. "What do you think you'll buy with the money, Joel?" he said.

Joel shrugged. "I don't know."

Maybe something for his guitar, he thought later. But right then, he didn't think he needed anything. He had his family and some friends and he was part of Wilchna.